W9-AAE-480

Here's what kids have to say to
Mary Pope Osborne, author of
the Magic Tree House series:

I never ever read that much until I read the Magic Tree House books, and after I read your books, I got started on reading. I read more and more. . . . Keep on writing, and I will keep on reading.—Seth L.

I had one of your books and I couldn't put it down!!! I really, really love your books.—Liza L.

I'm really enjoying your Magic Tree House books. They are my favorite books. . . . Today I had to write about three people I want to have come over for dinner. The three people I chose are Thomas Jefferson, Nicolas Cage, and, you guessed it, Mary Pope Osborne.—Will B.

I have read every single book you've written. . . . I love your books so much I would go wacko if you stopped writing your books.—Stephanie Z.

Once I start one [of your books], I never put it down until it is done. Your books make me feel like I am really in the place that Jack and Annie are in. When I read one of your books, I learn so many interesting new facts. Your books are the best!—Eliza D.

Parents and teachers love
Magic Tree House books, too!

I am the mother of four young sons who are thoroughly enjoying the adventures of Jack and Annie! We eagerly await each new release! We also use your books as Christmas and birthday gifts for friends and cousins—a welcome gift for the children and their parents!—C. Anders

We overheard the children in the schoolyard talking and laughing about "special friends." Upon further investigation, those friends turned out to be none other than Jack and Annie. These children have become devoted fans of your books. As parents, it is inspiring to see our children so absorbed in books.
—M. Knepper and P. Contessa

The library soon will have a new addition— something that I have dreamed of for a long time—a real wooden Magic Tree House and a beautiful tree mural to accompany it. . . . There are many Magic Tree House experts in every class. It's wonderful to see their enthusiasm and their eagerness to read the books.—R. Locke

Midnight on the Moon

by Mary Pope Osborne

illustrated by Sal Murdocca

A STEPPING STONE BOOK™

Random House 🏠 New York

For Jacob and Elena Levi
and Aram and Molly Hanessian

Text copyright © 1996 by Mary Pope Osborne.
Illustrations copyright © 1996 by Sal Murdocca.
All rights reserved under International and Pan-American Copyright
Conventions. Published in the United States by Random House, Inc., New York,
and simultaneously in Canada by Random House of Canada Limited, Toronto.

www.randomhouse.com/kids

Library of Congress Cataloging-in-Publication Data
Osborne, Mary Pope. Midnight on the moon / by Mary Pope Osborne ;
illustrated by Sal Murdocca.
   p. cm. — (Magic tree house ; #8) "A first stepping stone book."
SUMMARY: The magic tree house takes Jack and Annie to a moon base in the future
where they continue to search for the fourth thing they need to free their friend
Morgan from the magician's spell.
ISBN 978-0-679-86374-8 (trade)—ISBN 978-0-679-96374-5 (lib. bdg.)
[1. Moon—Fiction. 2. Time travel—Fiction. 3. Magic—Fiction. 4. Science fiction.]
I. Murdocca, Sal, ill.   II. Title.   III. Series: Osborne, Mary Pope. Magic tree house
series ; #8. PZ7.O81167Mi 1996 [Fic]—dc20 96-17298

Printed in the United States of America 60

Random House, Inc.   New York, Toronto, London, Sydney, Auckland

Contents

Prologue

One summer day in Frog Creek, Pennsylvania, a mysterious tree house appeared in the woods.

Eight-year-old Jack and his seven-year-old sister, Annie, climbed into the tree house.

The tree house was filled with books and it was *magic*. It could go any place that was in a book. All Jack and Annie had to do was to point to a picture and wish to go there.

They visited dinosaurs, knights, an Egyptian queen, pirates, ninjas, and the Amazon rain forest.

Along the way, they discovered that the tree house belonged to Morgan le Fay. Morgan was a magical librarian from the time of King Arthur. She traveled through time and space, gathering books for her library.

One day, Jack and Annie found a note that said Morgan was under a spell. Jack and Annie set out in the magic tree house to find four special things that would free her.

With the help of a mouse named Peanut, Jack and Annie found the first thing in old Japan, the second in the Amazon rain forest, and the third in the Ice Age.

Now Jack, Annie, and Peanut are ready to find the last thing . . . in *Midnight on the Moon*.

1

By Moonlight

"Jack!" whispered a voice.

Jack opened his eyes. He saw a figure in the moonlight.

"Wake up. Get dressed." It was his sister, Annie.

Jack turned on his lamp. He rubbed his eyes.

Annie was standing beside his bed. She wore jeans and a sweatshirt.

"Let's go to the tree house," she said.

"What time is it?" asked Jack. He put on his glasses.

"Don't look at your clock," said Annie.

Jack looked at his clock. "Oh, man," he said. "It's midnight. It's too dark."

"No, it isn't. The moon makes it bright enough to see," said Annie.

"Wait till morning," said Jack.

"No—now," said Annie. "We have to find the fourth M thing. I have a feeling that the full moon might help us."

"That's nuts," said Jack. "I want to sleep."

"You can sleep when we come back home," said Annie. "No time will have passed."

Jack sighed. "Oh, brother," he said.

But he got out of bed.

"Yay!" whispered Annie. "Meet you at the back door." She tiptoed out of Jack's room.

Jack yawned. He pulled on his jeans and sneakers and a sweatshirt. He put his notebook and pencil into his backpack. Then he crept down the stairs.

Annie opened the back door. Quietly, they stepped outside.

"Wait—" said Jack. "We need a flashlight."

"No, we don't. I told you—the moon will light our way," said Annie. And she took off.

Jack sighed, then followed her.

Annie was right, thought Jack. The moon was so bright that he could see his shadow. Everything seemed washed with silver.

Soon they left their street. Annie led the way into the Frog Creek woods. It was much darker under the shadows of the trees.

Jack looked up, searching for the tree house.

"There!" said Annie.

The magic tree house was shining in the moonlight.

Annie grabbed the rope ladder and started climbing up.

"Careful—go slowly," said Jack.

He followed her up the ladder and into the tree house.

Moonlight streamed through the window.

It shone on the letter M that shimmered on the wooden floor.

It shone on the three M things that rested on the M: a *moonstone* from the time of the ninjas, a *mango* from the Amazon rain forest, and a *mammoth bone* from the Ice Age.

"We need just one more M thing," said Annie, "to free Morgan from her spell."

Squeak.

"Peanut!" said Annie.

In the dim light, Jack saw a tiny mouse. She sat on an open book.

"You didn't expect to see us this late, did you?" said Annie.

She picked up Peanut. And Jack picked up the open book.

"So where are we going this time?" Annie asked him.

Jack held the book up to the moonlight.

"Uh-oh," he said. "I knew we should have brought a flashlight. I can't read a thing."

He could make out diagrams and shadowy pictures. But he couldn't read a word.

"Look at the cover," said Annie.

The letters were bigger on the cover. Jack squinted at them.

"It's called *Hello, Moon*," he said.

Annie gasped. "We're going to the moon?"

"Of course not," said Jack. "It's impossible to go to the moon without tons of equipment."

"Why?"

"There's no air. We couldn't breathe. Not only that, we'd boil to death if it was day and freeze to death if it was night."

"Yikes," said Annie. "So where do you think we are going?"

"Maybe a place where people train to be astronauts," said Jack.

"That sounds neat," said Annie.

"Yeah," said Jack. He'd always wanted to meet astronauts and space scientists.

"So say the wish," said Annie.

Jack opened the book again. He pointed to a picture of a dome-shaped structure.

"I wish we could go there," he said.

The wind started to blow.

The tree house started to spin.

It spun faster and faster and faster.

Then everything was silent.

Absolutely silent. As quiet and still as silence could be.

2
Space Motel

Jack opened his eyes.

He looked out the window. The tree house had landed inside a large white room.

"What kind of training place is this?" asked Annie.

"I don't know," said Jack.

The room was round. It had no windows. It had white floors and a curved wall lit by bright lights.

"Hello!" Annie called.

There was no answer.

Where were all the astronauts and space scientists? Jack wondered.

"There's nobody here," said Annie.

"How do you know?" said Jack.

"I just feel it," said Annie.

"We'd better find out where we are," said Jack.

He looked at the page in the moon book. He read the words below the picture of the dome.

> A moon base was built on the moon in the year 2031. The top of the dome slides open to let spacecrafts enter and leave.

"Oh, man—" Jack whispered.

"What's wrong?" said Annie.

Jack's heart pounded with excitement. He could hardly speak. "We've landed inside a moon base," he said.

"So...?" said Annie.

"So the moon base is on the moon!" said Jack.

Annie's eyes widened. "We're *on* the moon?" she asked.

Jack nodded. "The book says the moon base was built in the year 2031," he said. "So this book was written *after* that! Which means this book is from the *future!*"

"Oh, wow," said Annie. "Morgan must have gone forward in time to borrow it from a future library."

"Right," said Jack. "And now we're in the future, on the moon."

Squeak, squeak!

Annie and Jack looked at Peanut. The mouse was running around in circles.

"Poor Peanut," said Annie.

She tried to pick the mouse up. But Peanut hid behind the mango on the letter M.

"Maybe she's nervous about being on the moon," said Annie.

"She's not the only one," said Jack. He let out a deep breath, then he pushed his glasses into place.

"So what's a moon base?" asked Annie.

Jack looked at the book. He read aloud:

> When scientists visit the moon for short periods, they eat and sleep in the moon base.

"A space motel!" said Annie.

"I guess," said Jack. He read more:

The small base has a landing chamber
and a room for storing spacesuits.
Air and temperature controls make
breathing possible.

"So that's why we can breathe," Jack said.

"Let's explore," said Annie. "We have to find the fourth thing for Morgan."

"No, first we should study this map," said Jack. He pulled out his notebook.

"*You* study it," said Annie.

Jack copied the map. Then he drew in the tree house.

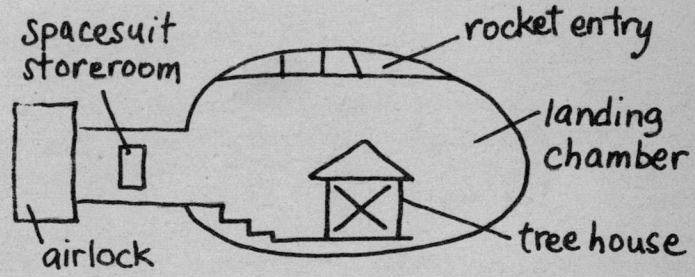

"Okay," he said. He pointed at the X in his drawing. "We're *here*."

Jack looked up. Annie was gone.

"Oh, brother," Jack said. As usual, she had left without him. Before they could even make a plan.

Jack put the moon book and pencil into his pack. Carrying his notebook and backpack, he started out the window.

Squeak! Squeak!

Jack looked back at Peanut. The mouse was running back and forth on the M.

"Stay here and be safe," said Jack. "We'll be back soon."

Jack swung himself over the window sill. His feet touched the floor of the landing chamber.

"Annie!" he called.

There was no answer.

Jack looked at his diagram.

It showed only one way to go. Jack walked along the curved white wall to the stairs.

He climbed the steps to a hallway.

"Jack—hurry!" Annie was at the end of the hallway, standing in the airlock. She peered out a window in a giant door.

Jack hurried toward her. Annie stepped aside so he could look out the window, too.

"Oh, man," said Jack. What he saw took his breath away.

He stared at a rocky gray land. The land was filled with giant craters and tall mountains. The sun was shining. But the sky was ink-black!

"Say hi to the moon," Annie said softly.

3

Open Sesame!

"The fourth M thing must be out there," said Annie.

Beside the door was a button with the word OPEN on it. Annie reached for the button.

"Wait!" Jack grabbed her hand. "There's no air on the moon. Remember?"

"Oh. Right. But we have to go out to find the M thing."

"Let's see what the book says," said Jack.

He pulled the book out of his pack. He flipped through it until he found a page that showed the surface of the moon. He read aloud:

> It takes fourteen Earth days to equal
> one day on the moon. No air protects
> the moon from the sun's rays, so
> daytime heat reaches 260 degrees.

Jack looked at Annie. "I told you our blood would boil if we went out there," he said.

"Yuck," she said.

Jack read from the book again:

> Moon scientists wear spacesuits,
> which have controls to keep them
> from getting too hot or too cold. They
> have tanks, which provide air for two
> hours.

"Where do we get spacesuits?" asked Annie. She looked around then trotted back down the hall. "Maybe there...?"

Jack was studying his map. "Let's try the spacesuit storeroom."

"Don't look at the map," said Annie. "Look at the *real* room!"

Jack glanced up. Annie was peering through a doorway off the hall.

"There's a ton of space stuff in here!" she said.

Jack went to look.

Bulky white suits hung from hangers. Air tanks, helmets, gloves, and boots sat in neat rows on shelves.

"Wow, it's like the armor room in a castle," said Jack.

"Yeah, with huge armor," said Annie.

"Let's pick out the smallest stuff," said Jack. "The suits can go over our clothes."

Annie found the smallest white suit. And Jack found the next smallest. They stepped into them.

Then Annie locked Jack's air tank into place.

"Thanks," he said. And he did the same for her.

"Thanks," she said.

"Gloves?" said Jack. He and Annie pulled on white gloves.

"Boots?" said Annie. They each pulled on a pair of huge white boots.

"Helmets?" said Jack. He reached for a helmet.

"Wow, they're pretty light," he said. "I thought they'd be like knights' helmets."

Jack and Annie put the helmets on. They locked each other's into place.

"I can't move my head right or left," said Annie.

"Me neither," said Jack. "Let's try walking."

Jack and Annie moved clumsily around the room. Jack felt like a fat snowman.

"Close your visor," said Annie.

They both closed their see-through visors. Cool air filled Jack's helmet.

"I CAN BREATHE!" Annie yelled. Her voice boomed in Jack's ears.

"Ow! Talk quietly," Jack said. "We have two-way radios inside our helmets."

"Sorry," whispered Annie.

Jack put the moon book back in his pack. Then he slung the pack over his shoulder.

"Okay!" he said. "Remember, we only have two hours of air in our tanks. So we need to find the fourth M thing really fast."

"I hope we can find it," said Annie.

"Me too," said Jack. He knew they could not go home until they did.

"Let's go," said Annie. She gave Jack a little push.

"Watch it. No goofing off," he said. "We don't want to fall over in these suits."

"Just go—go!" said Annie. She pushed him out of the room. They walked back to the airlock.

"Ready?" said Annie. "Open sesame!" She pressed the OPEN button. A door slowly slid closed behind them. A door opened in front of them.

And Jack and Annie stepped out onto the moon.

4
Moon Rabbits

"Oh, wow!" said Annie. She took a step forward.

But Jack stood frozen. He wanted to get a good look at everything first.

He stared at the ground. He was standing in a layer of gray dust as fine as powder.

Footprints were everywhere. Jack wondered who had made them.

He reached into his pack for the moon book. To his surprise, it was as light as a feather!

He found a picture of footprints on the moon. He read:

> The moon has no rain or wind to blow the dust around. So footprints will never wear away naturally, not even in a billion years.

"Oh, man," Jack said.

The moon was the stillest place he had ever, *ever* been. It was as still as a picture. And its stillness would never, ever end.

Jack stared at the ink-black sky. A lovely blue-and-white ball glowed far away.

Earth.

For the first time, it really hit Jack. They were in outer space.

"Look!" Annie cried, laughing.

She bounded past Jack—almost flying

through the air. She landed on her feet. Then she jumped again.

"I'm a moon rabbit," she called.

Jack laughed. How does she do that? he wondered. He turned a page and read:

> A person weighs less on the moon because of the moon's low gravity and lack of air. If you weigh 60 pounds on Earth, you would only weigh 10 pounds on the moon.

"Don't just stand there reading!" said Annie, grabbing the book from Jack's gloved hand. She tossed it into space.

It flew far away.

Jack started after it.

He bounded up and down. *Boing! Boing! Boing!* Now *he* felt as light as a feather.

"Look!" he called to Annie. "I'm a moon rabbit, too."

Where Jack's boots hit the ground, moon-dust gracefully sprayed into space.

The book had landed at the edge of a shallow crater.

When Jack reached it, he tried to stop. But his feet slipped.

He fell right over and lay on his side. He tried to stand. But he was off-balance.

He tried again. But the dust was just too deep. And his spacesuit was too clumsy.

"You okay?" asked Annie.

"I can't get up," said Jack.

"You shouldn't have been goofing off," said Annie wisely.

"You goofed off first," said Jack. "Now, help me up, please."

Annie started toward him.

"Don't fall, too," warned Jack.

"I won't." Annie moved very slowly. She half floated, half walked.

"Give me your hand," she said.

Annie grabbed Jack's hand. She pressed her boot against his and pulled him up.

"Thanks," he said.

"No problem," she said. "It was easy. You were really light."

"Thank goodness," said Jack. "It's impossible to get up alone."

He picked up the moon book. It was covered with dust. He brushed it off.

"Oh, wow! Look!" said Annie. She stood at the edge of the crater.

"What is it?" said Jack.

"A moon buggy!" said Annie.

The buggy was parked in the crater. It had four huge wheels.

"Let's go for a ride," said Annie.

"We can't," said Jack. "We just have two hours of air in our tanks. Remember?"

"I bet we'll find the M thing faster if we take the moon buggy!" Annie bounded into the crater.

"But we can't drive!" said Jack.

"I bet I can drive *this*," said Annie. "It looks easy. Come on!"

She jumped into the driver's seat.

"But you don't have a license!" said Jack.

"Who cares?" said Annie. "There aren't any roads on the moon, or stoplights, or policemen either."

She was right, Jack thought.

"Well, go slow," he said. And he climbed in beside her.

Annie pushed a button labeled ON.

The moon buggy lurched backward.

"Yikes!" said Annie.

"Step on the brake!" said Jack.

Annie pressed a pedal on the floor. The buggy stopped with a jerk.

"Whew," she said.

"It must be in reverse," said Jack. "Let me study this—"

But before he could study anything, Annie pushed another button.

The buggy tilted back. Its front wheels started to rise into the air.

"Let me out of here!" said Jack.

Annie pushed more buttons.

The buggy's front wheels landed back on the ground. And the buggy leaped forward.

"*Slower!*" said Jack.

"I can't," said Annie. "I don't know how!"

Annie steered the buggy over the tracks on the ground. The wide wheels kept it from sinking into the deep dust.

"Careful!" said Jack.

The buggy zoomed out of the crater.

Gray clouds of dust rose behind them as they took off across the moon.

5
Hang On!

Annie drove the moon buggy over bumps and hollows. It bucked like a bronco.

"I'm going through *there*!" She pointed to an opening between two mountains.

Jack held on to the dashboard.

The buggy bumped toward the opening and shot through.

On the other side, the ground was even rockier.

"Look for the fo-fourth M thing!" said Annie, bouncing up and down.

Jack groaned. Looking for anything on this wild ride was impossible.

"Sl-slow d-down!" he said.

"How?"

"Try pressing on the b-brake pedal. On the f-floor—slowly!"

Annie pressed on the brake.

The buggy slowed down. Jack sighed with

relief. The ride was still bumpy. But now, at least, he could take a good look at the moon.

He had never been to such a colorless, barren place. There was no green, no blue, no red.

No water, no trees, no clouds.

Only giant gray rocks and craters—*and an American flag.*

"Oh, man," said Jack. "That's from the first astronauts who landed on the moon!"

"And look—a telescope!" said Annie.

She drove near the flag and telescope. Then she put her foot on the brake until the buggy stopped.

She pressed a button that said OFF. Then she and Jack hopped out.

They took slow giant steps to the site of the first moon landing.

Beside the flag was a sign. Annie read it aloud:

HERE MEN FROM THE PLANET EARTH
FIRST SET FOOT UPON THE MOON,
JULY 1969 A.D.
WE CAME IN PEACE
FOR ALL MANKIND.

"That's a good message," said Jack.

He handed the moon book to Annie. Then he took out his notebook and pencil to copy the sign.

"Let's leave our own message," said Annie.

"What should we say?" said Jack.

"The same thing," said Annie. "But say we are the first kids."

Jack turned to a new page in his notebook. In big letters he wrote their message.

"Now we have to sign it," Annie said.

Jack signed his name.

Then he passed the notebook and pencil to Annie. She signed her name and passed the notebook back.

Jack tore out the piece of paper. He put it by the flag.

> Today the first kids from the planet
> Earth came to the Moon. We came in
> peace for all children.
>
> Jack
>
> ANNIE

No wind would ever blow the message away. No rain would ever fall on it.

It would be there forever, unless someone moved it.

Thinking of "forever" made Jack feel dizzy. He shook his head to clear his thoughts. Then he remembered the time. Had two hours passed yet?

"I wish I had a watch," he said, standing up. "We might be running out of time."

"Oh, wow. A moon man!" said Annie.

"What?" Jack turned to look at her.

She was staring through the telescope.

Jack walked over to the telescope. Annie stepped aside so he could look, too.

Jack gasped. In the distance, something was flying above the ground.

It looked like a giant man in a spacesuit.

6
High Jump

"Who is *that?*" said Jack.

"I don't know," said Annie. "But we'll soon find out!" She started waving.

"No!" said Jack. He grabbed her arm. "Let's go back to the base—before he gets here!"

"Why?" said Annie.

"We don't know who he is!" said Jack. "We don't know if he's friendly or mean or what."

"But we can't go back," said Annie. "We haven't found the fourth M thing yet.

We won't be able to go home."

"It doesn't matter. We can lock the door at the moon base until he goes away," said Jack. "Then we can get new air tanks!"

Jack hurried to the moon buggy. "Come on!" He jumped into the driver's seat.

Annie gave a little wave to the dot in the sky. Then she climbed into the moon buggy.

The buggy took off.

"Careful!" said Annie.

They bumped over the rocks as Jack turned the buggy around. Then they zoomed toward the pass.

Jack steered around craters and rocks. More than once the buggy nearly tipped over.

"Whoa! Slow down!" said Annie.

They were almost at the mountain pass. Suddenly, a cloud of dust flew up in front of them. The ground trembled.

"Watch it!" cried Annie.

Jack couldn't see a thing.

He stepped on the brake. The buggy jerked to a stop.

The dust settled.

A giant rock had fallen into the narrow pass. It was stuck between two walls of rock. They were trapped!

Jack quickly found a picture of a giant rock in the moon book. He read aloud:

> Rocks of all sizes crash into the moon
> from outer space. These rocks are
> called meteorites.

"We're lucky that meteorite didn't land on *us*," said Jack.

"Yeah, and I guess it's too big to be the M thing," said Annie. She had climbed out of the moon buggy and was standing by the meteorite.

It was more than twice as tall as she was.

Jack looked at the black sky. The flying thing was nowhere in sight—yet.

"We'll have to jump over it," Annie said.

"Jump? I don't think so," said Jack. "It's too high."

"I'm going to try anyway," said Annie.

"Wait. Let's think first," said Jack.

But Annie was already backing up.

"One, two, three—go!" she shouted, and took giant, leaping steps toward the meteorite.

When Annie got close to the rock, she pushed off the ground. Then she flew through space and disappeared behind the meteorite.

"Annie!" Jack called.

There was no answer.

"Oh, brother," Jack said. He backed up and took off toward the rock. He jumped as high as he could. Then he was flying through space.

Jack hit the ground and fell facedown into the dust.

Jack tried to stand. But his suit was too bulky. He tried to roll over. But his suit made even that impossible.

"Oh, no," he groaned. "Not again."

"Are you here?" asked Annie. "Did you make it?"

"Yes!" Jack was relieved to hear her voice. But he couldn't turn his head to see her. He could only hear her over the radio.

"Can you help me up?" he asked.

"Nope," said Annie.

"Why not?"

"I fell down, too," she said.

"Oh, brother," Jack sighed. "Now we are *really* in trouble."

He tried to stand again. And failed.

"Can you see anything?" he asked.

"Just the sky," said Annie. "Wow, is it weird..."

"I'm worried about our air tanks," said Jack. "I feel like it's been two hours."

"Ja-ack..." said Annie.

"And what about that moon man?" said Jack. "Where did he go to?"

"Jack!" whispered Annie.

"What?"

"He's here," she said. "The moon man is here."

"*What?*"

"He's standing above me."

7

The Moon Man

Jack's heart nearly stopped.

He could hear Annie talking.

"Hi," she said. "We come in peace."

There was silence. Then Jack heard Annie say, "Thank you. I have to help my brother up now."

A moment later, Annie rolled Jack onto his back.

She grabbed his hand and pulled him up.

"Thanks," said Jack, once he was standing.

The moon man was a few feet away. His

face was hidden by a metal visor.

He looked like a spaceman. A *huge* spaceman—with a giant tank on his back. It was as big as a refrigerator.

"That's a jet pack!" said Jack. "I've seen pictures of future astronauts flying with those things. It's like a mini-spaceship. Right?"

The moon man didn't answer.

"I don't think he can hear us," said Annie. "He's not hooked up to our radio."

"Oh, right," said Jack. "I'll write him a message!"

"Good idea," said Annie.

Jack pulled out his notebook and pencil. He wrote:

We're Jack and Annie. We come in peace from America. Who are you?

Jack handed the notebook and his pencil to the moon man. They looked tiny in his big hands.

The moon man looked down at the message. He looked at the tiny pencil. Then he turned the notebook over.

Jack and Annie watched as the moon man put the pencil to the paper. He was writing something very carefully.

Finally he gave the notebook back to Jack.

Jack and Annie stared at the marks.

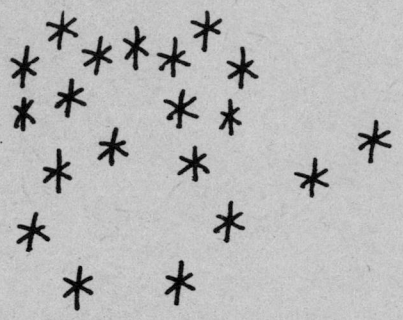

"Stars," said Annie. "He drew stars."

"Maybe it's a space map," said Jack.

"Space map?" said Annie. "Hey, Jack, *map* starts with M!"

"Oh, wow," said Jack. "This must be the fourth M thing!"

"Let's ask him what his map means," said Annie. She turned around.

"We'll never know now," she said.

"Why?" Jack looked up from the map.

"That's why." Annie pointed. The moon man was flying over the mountains.

"Thanks!" Annie cried.

8

One Star to Another

"Who *was* that guy?" said Jack. "What does his map mean?"

"I don't know," said Annie. "But let's see if it works."

Jack took a deep breath. "Yeah, we'd better hurry back. I think I'm running out of air. It feels harder to breathe."

"For me, too," said Annie.

"Go slow. Don't breathe too much," said Jack.

He and Annie took long, floating steps

toward the moon base. Jack held his breath as if he were underwater.

By the time they got to the white dome, he was ready to burst.

Annie pushed a button beside the huge door. It slid open. They hurried into the airlock. The door closed behind them and the door to the hallway opened.

Jack opened the visor of his helmet. He took a long, deep breath—and let it out. "Ahhhh!"

"Let's get out of these suits," said Annie.

"Good idea." Jack was dying to free his arms and legs.

As they moved clumsily into the spacesuit storeroom, Jack felt heavy again.

He and Annie unlocked each other's helmets, gloves, and boots, and pulled everything off. Then they stepped out of their bulky suits.

"Whew!" Jack said. He took off his glasses and rubbed his eyes.

It was great to be free—even if he no longer felt as light as a feather.

"Hurry! Peanut's waiting!" said Annie.

She led the way down the steps to the bright landing chamber.

"Yay," she said softly.

Jack was relieved to see the tree house still there. Soon they'd be heading home. He couldn't wait.

Jack and Annie crawled through the tree house window.

"We're back, Peanut!" said Annie.

Squeak! Peanut ran to the letter M.

"We missed you!" said Annie. She patted

the mouse's head. "We met a moon man."

"Sorry, Peanut, but you have to move," said Jack. "We have to put the map on the M."

Annie gently lifted the mouse off the M.

Jack tore the star map out of his notebook. He placed it on the M, next to the mammoth bone, the mango, and the moonstone.

He sighed, then sat back on his heels. "Hand me the Pennsylvania book," he said. They needed the Pennsylvania book to get back home.

There was silence.

Jack turned and looked at Annie.

"It's not working, Jack," she said. "The book's not here."

"What?" Was the map the wrong thing?

They looked around the tree house.

"It's definitely not here," said Annie.

"Oh, no." Jack's heart sank. He picked up the star map and stared at it.

Squeak, squeak. Peanut jumped out of Annie's arms and scurried back to the letter M.

"I've got an idea," said Jack. He reached

into his pack and took out his pencil.

"What are you doing?" said Annie.

"You know how you draw a constellation?" said Jack. "You connect all the stars. What happens if we try that?"

He drew a line from one star to another. He kept drawing, until all the stars were connected.

"Let me see," said Annie.

Jack held the paper out so they could both study it.

"It looks like a mouse," said Annie.

"Yeah," said Jack.

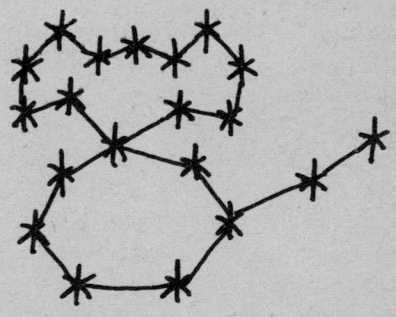

"Is there such a thing as a mouse constellation?" said Annie.

"I don't think so..." said Jack.

Squeak.

Annie and Jack looked at Peanut. She was standing on the M.

"Oh, wow. Jack," Annie whispered, "I think I know what the fourth thing is—"

Jack grinned. "Me too," he said. "It's a—"

"*Mouse!*" they said together.

Squeak! Squeak!

"Maybe the spell is—*Moonstone, mango, mammoth bone, mouse!*" said Annie.

Jack touched each M thing in turn as he whispered, "Moonstone, mango, mammoth bone, mouse."

"Let's say it over and over and see what happens," said Annie.

Together, they chanted:

*"Moonstone, mango,
  mammoth bone, mouse.
  Moonstone, mango,
  mammoth bone, mouse."*

Suddenly, a bright light filled the tree house.

The light got brighter and brighter and brighter.

The brightness was blinding and whirling.

The air spun with brightness.

Then everything was clear.

Peanut the mouse was gone.

And Morgan le Fay stood before Jack and Annie.

9

Morgan

"Thank you," Morgan said softly. "You have freed me from the magician's spell."

Jack just stared at her.

"*You* were Peanut?" Annie said.

Morgan nodded and smiled.

"Really? You were with us all the time?" said Jack. "On all our missions?"

Morgan nodded again.

"Why did we have to go on this mission to find a mouse?" said Jack. "If you were always with us?"

"To break the spell, we had to be on the moon," said Morgan. "You could have broken it the minute we arrived."

"Oh, that's what Peanut—I mean *you* were trying to say!" said Annie. "We didn't have to leave the moon base at all."

Morgan nodded, smiling.

"But the moon man came along to help us," said Annie. "He drew a constellation of a mouse! Is he a friend of yours?"

Morgan shrugged. "Let's just say we had a little talk. He stopped by the moon base while you were out."

"The same way you had a talk with the ninja master, right?" said Jack. "And the monkey and the sorcerer?"

Morgan nodded. "I always squeaked to the ones who helped you."

"But how did they understand you—a mouse?" said Jack.

Morgan smiled again. "Certain wise ones understand the language of little creatures," she said.

"I bet it was you who turned the pages of the books!" said Annie. "To show us where to go next!"

Morgan nodded.

"But who turned you into a mouse?" said Annie.

Morgan frowned. "A certain person who likes to play tricks on me," she said. "His name is Merlin."

"Merlin!" said Jack. "The greatest magician who ever lived."

Morgan sniffed. "He's not that great," she said. "He doesn't even know I have two brave friends who help me."

"Us?" said Annie shyly.

Morgan nodded. "And I thank you both with all my heart."

"You're welcome," said Jack and Annie.

Morgan handed Annie the Pennsylvania book. "Are you ready to go home now?" she asked.

"Yes!" said Jack and Annie.

Annie pointed to a picture of the Frog Creek woods. "I wish we could go there," she said.

The tree house started to spin.

It spun faster and faster and faster.

Then everything was still.

Absolutely still.

But only for a moment.

10

Earth Life

The midnight woods woke up.

A breeze rustled the leaves.

An owl hooted.

The sounds were soft, but very alive.

Jack opened his eyes. He pushed his glasses into place.

He smiled. Morgan was still with them. He could see her in the moonlight. Her long white hair was shining.

"Morgan, can you and the tree house stay

here?" said Annie. "In Frog Creek?"

"No, I must leave again, I'm afraid," said Morgan. "I've been gone from Camelot for a long time."

She handed Jack his pack. She brushed his cheek. Her hand felt soft and cool.

"A bit of moondust still on you," she said. "Thank you, Jack, for your great love of knowledge."

"You're welcome," said Jack.

Morgan tugged on one of Annie's braids. "And thank you, Annie, for your belief in the impossible."

"You're welcome," said Annie.

"Go home now," said Morgan.

Jack smiled. Home was Earth—that bright, colorful world where everything was alive and always changing.

"Bye, Morgan," said Annie. She started out of the tree house.

Jack looked back at Morgan.

"Will you come back soon?" he said.

"Anything can happen," said Morgan. "The universe is filled with wonders. Isn't it, Jack?"

He smiled and nodded.

"Go now," Morgan said softly.

Jack followed Annie down the rope ladder. He stepped onto the ground.

The wind started to blow.

The tree started to shake.

A loud roar filled Jack's ears. He squeezed his eyes shut. He covered his ears.

Then everything was silent and still.

Jack opened his eyes. The ladder was gone. He looked through the leaves and branches of the giant oak tree. Where the tree house had been was only moonlight now.

"Bye, Morgan," he whispered sadly.

"Bye, Peanut," said Annie.

Jack and Annie stared at the top of the tree for a long moment.

"Ready?" said Annie.

Jack nodded.

They started for home.

The midnight air felt cool and moist. It was filled with the soft sounds of earth life.

Jack and Annie left the Frog Creek woods. They started down their street.

Annie glanced up at the sky. "The moon looks really far away, doesn't it?"

It did, thought Jack. It *was*.

"I wonder how the moon man can be up there all alone," said Annie.

"What do you mean?" said Jack.

"I mean, who helps him put on his space-suit?" said Annie. "Who helps him get up when he falls down?"

"And who is he?" added Jack.

"Who do you think he was?" said Annie.

"He must be a scientist or an astronaut from Earth," said Jack.

"No. I think he's an alien," said Annie, "from another galaxy."

Jack scoffed. "What makes you say that?"

"I just feel it," said Annie.

"Wrong," said Jack. "There's no proof that aliens exist."

"Maybe not now," said Annie. "But don't forget—we were in the future."

"Oh, brother," said Jack.

They crossed their yard and climbed their

back steps. Annie tiptoed inside the house. Jack followed her.

Before he shut the door, he glanced up at the moon.

Was Annie right? he wondered. Could the moon man have come from another galaxy?

Morgan's words came back to him: *The universe is filled with wonders. Isn't it, Jack?*

"Goodnight, moon man," Jack whispered. Then he closed the door.

Want to learn more about space?

Get the facts behind the fiction in the Magic Tree House® Research Guide.

Available now!

Get your
Official
Magic Tree House
PASSPORT!
www.magictreehouse.com

Around the World with Jack and Annie!

You have traveled to far away places and have been
on countless Magic Tree House adventures.
Now is your chance to receive an official
Magic Tree House passport and collect official stamps
for each destination from around the world!

HOW

Get your exclusive Magic Tree House Passport!*

Send your name, street address, city, state, zip code, and date of birth to:
The Magic Tree House Passport, Random House Children's Books,
Marketing Department, 1745 Broadway, 10th Floor, New York, NY 10019

OR log on to **www.magictreehouse.com/passport**
to download and print your passport now!

Collect Official Magic Tree House Stamps:

Log on to **www.magictreehouse.com** to submit your answer to the
trivia questions below. If you answer correctly, you will automatically
receive your official stamp for Book 8: *Midnight on the Moon.*

1. When scientists visit the moon where do they eat and sleep?

2. What did Jack and Annie find sticking out
of the giant gray rocks and craters?

3. What was the fourth "M" thing Jack and Annie needed
to find in order to complete the spell?

Read all the Magic Tree House adventures for a chance to collect them all!

Don't miss the next Magic Tree House book, in which Jack and Annie are whisked out to sea and find both dolphins *and* sharks . . .

MAGIC TREE HOUSE® #9

DOLPHINS AT DAYBREAK

Guess what?
Jack and Annie have a musical CD!

For more information about
MAGIC TREE HOUSE: THE MUSICAL
(including how to order the CD!),
visit www.mthmusical.com.

SUPER RABBIT BOY
BLASTS OFF!

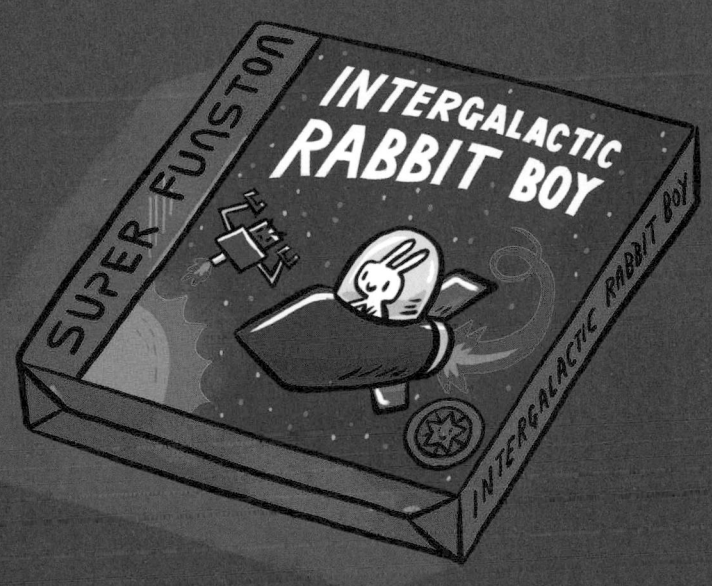

READ MORE
PRESS START!
BOOKS!

MORE BOOKS COMING SOON!

PRESS START!

SUPER RABBIT BOY BLASTS OFF!

THOMAS FLINTHAM

BRANCHES

SCHOLASTIC INC.

FOR GEMMA AND STEVE

Copyright © 2018 by Thomas Flintham

All rights reserved. Published by Scholastic Inc., *Publishers since 1920.* SCHOLASTIC, BRANCHES, and associated logos are trademarks and/or registered trademarks of Scholastic Inc.

The publisher does not have any control over and does not assume any responsibility for author or third-party websites or their content.

No part of this publication may be reproduced, stored in a retrieval system, or transmitted in any form or by any means, electronic, mechanical, photocopying, recording, or otherwise, without written permission of the publisher. For information regarding permission, write to Scholastic Inc., Attention: Permissions Department, 557 Broadway, New York, NY 10012.

This book is a work of fiction. Names, characters, places, and incidents are either the product of the author's imagination or are used fictitiously, and any resemblance to actual persons, living or dead, business establishments, events, or locales is entirely coincidental.

Library of Congress Cataloging-in-Publication Data

Name: Flintham, Thomas, author, illustrator. | Flintham, Thomas. Press start!
Title: Super Rabbit Boy blasts off! / by Thomas Flintham.
Description: First edition. | New York : Branches/Scholastic Inc., 2018. |
Series: Press start! ; 5 | Summary: King Viking decides to find another
planet where he can carry out his evil plans without interference, and
everyone in Animal Town is delighted; then an alien appeals to Super
Rabbit Boy for help and he blasts off to once again confront his
enemy—but his level one rocket may not be up to the task.
Identifiers: LCCN 2017048081 | ISBN 9781338239706 (hardcover) |
ISBN 9781338239621 (pbk.)
Subjects: LCSH: Superheroes—Juvenile fiction. | Supervillains—Juvenile
fiction. | Animals—Juvenile fiction. | Space ships—Juvenile fiction. |
Video games—Juvenile fiction. | CYAC: Superheroes—Fiction. |
Supervillains—Fiction. | Animals—Fiction. | Space ships—Fiction. |
Video games—Fiction.
Classification: LCC PZ7.1.F585 Sr 2018 | DDC [Fic]—dc23
LC record available at https://lccn.loc.gov/2017048081

10 9 8 7 6 5 4 3 2 1   18 19 20 21 22

Printed in China   38
First edition, August 2018
Edited by Celia Lee
Book design by Maria Mercado

TABLE OF CONTENTS

1 PRESS START!

This is Animal Town. Hero Super Rabbit Boy and all his friends are having a party! Main meanie, King Viking, has gone away forever.

He left this letter for Super Rabbit Boy.

DEAR <u>STINKY</u> RABBIT BOY,

  I HAVE HAD ENOUGH.
YOU WIN! YOU ALWAYS RUIN
MY BEST PLANS AND BEAT MY
BEST ROBOTS. I AM MOVING AWAY.
  I AM BLASTING OFF INTO SPACE,
AND I AM NEVER COMING BACK. I WANT
TO BE FAR AWAY FROM YOU AND ALL
YOUR HAPPY FRIENDS.
  I HOPE YOU HAVE A BAD LIFE!

  YOURS SINCERELY,
  KING VIKING

P.S. I THINK SPACE WILL BE GREAT!

Everyone in Animal Town is so happy without King Viking! He won't destroy things ever again.

Suddenly, Celia Crocodile spots a spark in the sky.

Is that a shooting star?

No, it's a space rocket heading straight for Animal Town!

Animal Town is shocked that King Viking is causing trouble in space. But Super Rabbit Boy is ready.

3 . . . 2 . . . 1 . . . BLAST OFF!

Boing! Boing! Here I come!

2 UP, UP, AND AWAY!

Super Rabbit Boy is in space. Stars and planets are everywhere.

Wow, space is amazing!

Super Rabbit Boy starts his search for King Viking. But the rocket moves slowly.

Suddenly, he spots action up ahead.

It's an army of King Viking's Rocket-Robos.

BOOP! It's Super Rabbit Boy!

BEEP! What is he doing in space?

BEEP! BOOP! GET HIM!

12

Super Rabbit Boy swoops into action.

It's time to test out this rocket's laser!

LASER

He tests the laser on the zooming Rocket-Robos. They're hard to stop!

This is tricky!

The Level 1 rocket has a very weak laser. But Super Rabbit Boy learns how to make it work.

BEEP!

I'm getting the hang of this!

He needs to get the Rocket-Robos three times each to stop them.

BOOP!

Super Rabbit Boy stops the final Rocket-Robo. The whole army has been beaten!

Did I beat all of them?

Super Rabbit Boy sees a flash in the distance.

Wait, what is that?

It's a giant Rocket-Robo Boss! The Boss is attacking a space station with its laser cannons!

Super Rabbit Boy is ready. But his Level 1 rocket is so weak. The Rocket-Robo Boss is stronger than the Rocket-Robos. Will he be able to defeat the Rocket-Robo Boss?

Boing! Boing! Here I go!

Super Rabbit Boy zooms toward the Rocket-Robo Boss!

Stop that, you Robo bully!

No, I will not. BOOP!

The Rocket-Robo Boss fires its laser cannons at Super Rabbit Boy.

I will stop you, Super Rabbit Boy!

Super Rabbit Boy's Level 1 rocket is not very fast. But he still dodges the cannon blasts.

Super Rabbit Boy's laser finds the Rocket-Robo Boss. Nothing happens!

BOOP! BOOP! Your Level 1 laser is too weak for my Level 5 robot-armor!

Oh no! What can Super Rabbit Boy do? Suddenly, a voice calls out from the space station.

Super Rabbit Boy fires at the Rocket-Robo Boss's three glowing weak spots.

BOOP!

ZAP!

ZAP!

ZAP!

BEEP!

HOORAY!

You did it, Super Rabbit Boy!

The Flobs on the space station are happy!
They invite Super Rabbit Boy aboard to
thank him.

I know! We can upgrade your rocket to Level 2.
We hope it helps you on your journey!
That would be great! Thank you!

Soon, Super Rabbit Boy blasts off in search of King Viking. This time he's in a shiny, upgraded Level 2 rocket!

LEVEL 2
This is great! I'm much faster now.

Super Rabbit Boy approaches a red planet.

> **Maybe I'll find some sign of King Viking here. . . .**

Oh no! Another army of King Viking's Rocket-Robos is attacking the planet! Can Super Rabbit Boy save the red planet from King Viking's Rocket-Robo Army?

5 A BIG SURPRISE

Super Rabbit Boy swoops into action! His Level 2 rocket can stop each Rocket-Robo with just one blast!

Take that!

BOOP!

Super Rabbit Boy makes his way through the Rocket-Robo Army.

BEEP!

BOOP!

There are so many of them! I'm glad my rocket is now a Level 2!

BEEP!

The Rocket-Robos try to fire back at Super Rabbit Boy. But he's too fast now! He zooms out of the way.

Super Rabbit Boy is good at flying his upgraded rocket. He speeds easily through the army of Rocket-Robos.

Super Rabbit Boy chases the last of the Rocket-Robos down toward the surface of the red planet.

The small Roo-Roos watch as they fly toward them.

Don't worry! I am here to help.

The Roo-Roos cheer as Super Rabbit Boy beats the last of the Rocket-Robos.

Suddenly, a huge shadow falls over the red planet.

It is a huge Robo-U.F.O.!

Give me all of your metal!

Why does it need metal?

Oh no!

Eek!

34

6 INSIDE SPACE

Super Rabbit Boy circles around the giant Robo-U.F.O. He's looking for a weak spot. He can't find one. All of his blasts bounce off the armor.

BOOP! BOOP! My <u>Level 6</u> armor covers all my weak points. You can't beat me!

Super Rabbit Boy has an idea.

I know what to do!

He flies straight into the Robo-U.F.O.'s mouth!

Inside, he finds a maze of pipes. Super Rabbit Boy twists and turns as he searches for a weak spot!

There must be a weak spot somewhere.

Super Rabbit Boy sees a glow in one corner. He zooms toward it.

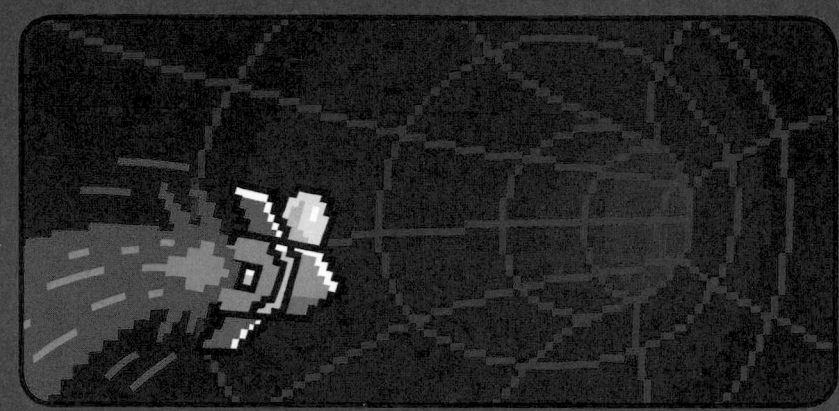

It's a giant room with a giant glowing core.

This must be the Robo-U.F.O.'s weak spot!

Super Rabbit Boy fires his laser at the glowing core.

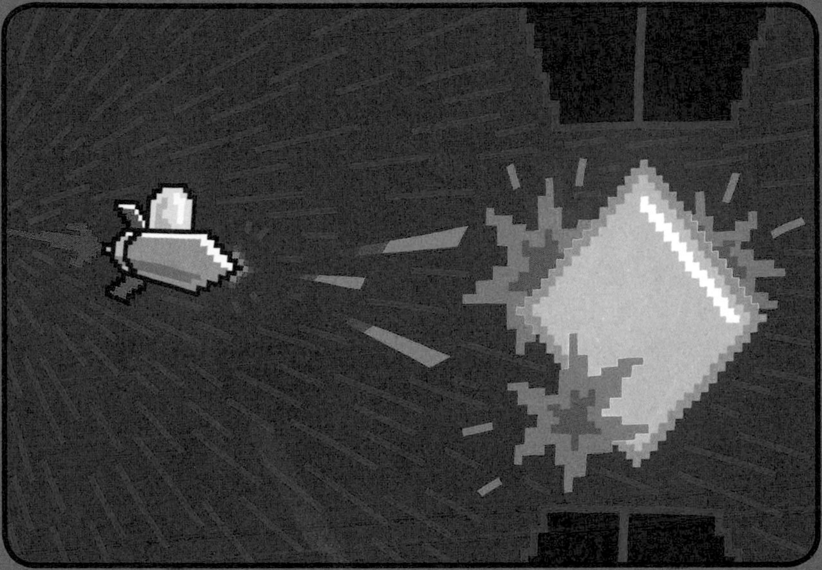

It takes a few tries, but the core breaks at last! The whole room starts to shake.

I better get out of here!

Super Rabbit Boy has to fly quickly back through the maze. Can he find his way out of the Robo-U.F.O. before it's too late?

Quick, Super Rabbit Boy!

Super Rabbit Boy's rocket flies out of the Robo-U.F.O. just in time! The Robo-U.F.O. explodes with a big bang!

BOOOOOOOP!

Good work, Super Rabbit Boy! You did it!

The Roo-Roos cheer! They are thankful, so they upgrade Super Rabbit Boy's rocket.

Now Super Rabbit Boy has a <u>Level 3</u> rocket! He sets off once again to search for King Viking.

LEVEL 3

Super Rabbit Boy flies near a blue moon.
He spies some more Rocket-Robos.

He quickly blasts his way through the
army. The Level 3 laser really helps!

After the army, Super Rabbit Boy sees another Rocket-Robo Boss. It's attacking a moon base full of Moonies.

This Rocket-Robo Boss has super long arms. It tries to grab Super Rabbit Boy's rocket. Super Rabbit Boy uses his Level 3 rocketspeed to fly out of the way.

Super Rabbit Boy sees the Rocket-Robo
Boss's glowing weak spot. He uses his laser.

The Rocket-Robo Boss blasts apart into many pieces!

I did it! Now I must find King Viking!

Oh no! How will Super Rabbit Boy ever catch up to and beat a Level 10 rocket?

8 THE SPACE CHASE

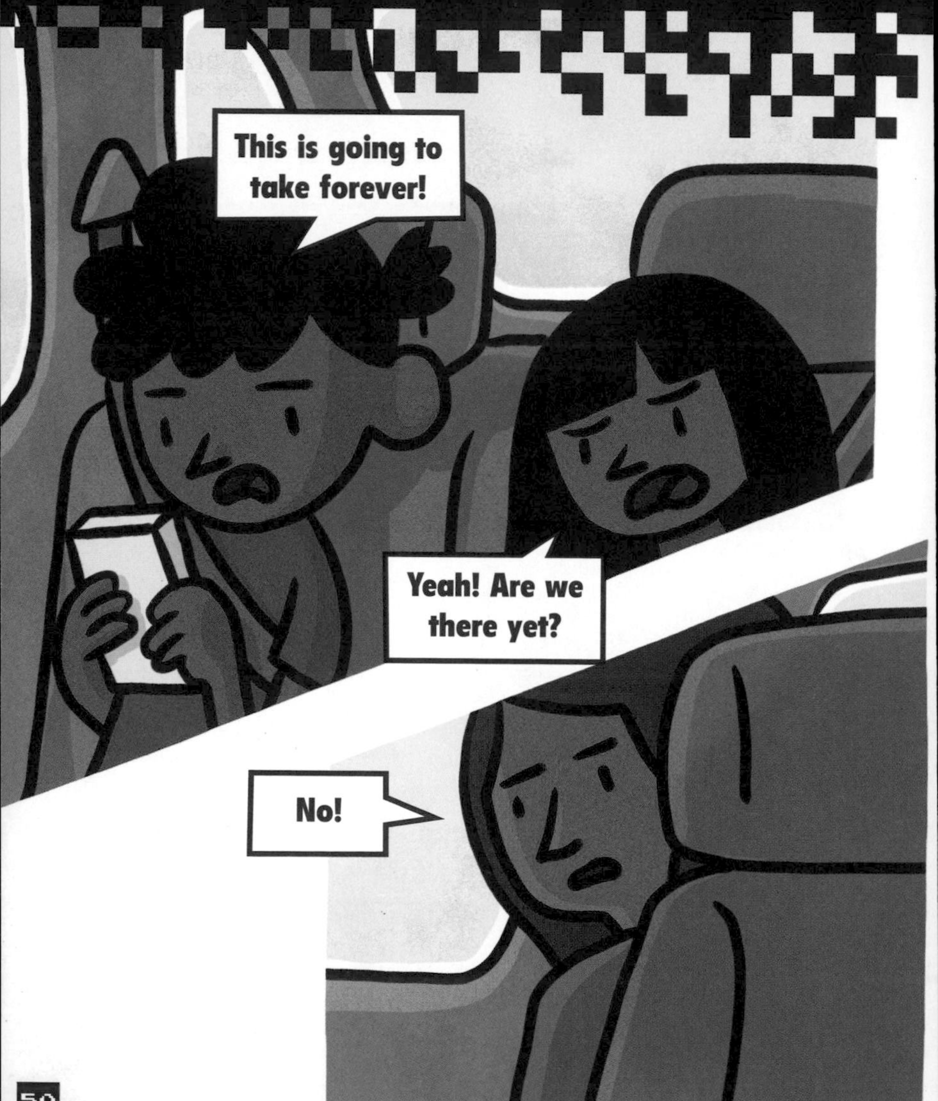

The Moonies thank Super Rabbit Boy for saving their moon base.

They upgrade Super Rabbit Boy's rocket to thank him. Now it's at Level 4!

Super Rabbit Boy keeps searching for King Viking and upgrading his rocket. He stops any Rocket-Robos he finds.

He stops any Rocket-Robo Bosses, too.

BOOP!

Are we there yet?

No!

Everywhere Super Rabbit Boy goes, there are more Rocket-Robos. But he does not see any sign of King Viking.

Now Super Rabbit Boy's search brings him to a space city. It is under attack by another Robo-U.F.O.

His Level 10 rocket is powerful! His laser goes straight through the Robo-U.F.O.'s armor in one blast!

57

Suddenly, someone taps Super Rabbit Boy on the back.

Yar! Excuse me, Super Rabbit Boy, I have a special gift for you!

Thank you! What is it?

Yar! It's my new machine! It can upgrade a rocket to Level 11!

Level 11? That means I'll be stronger than King Viking! Thank you!

Hooray! Keep going, Super Rabbit Boy!

9 SUPER SPEED

Super Rabbit Boy blasts off into space again. His Level 11 rocket is so fast! It moves at the speed of light.

I'll catch up with KIng Viking in no time!

LEVEL 11

Super Rabbit Boy finds a super big rocket zooming through space. Rocket-Robos fly out of the rocket toward him.

Super Rabbit Boy fires his Level 11 laser!

The Level 11 laser stops all the Rocket-Robos in one blast!

61

Super Rabbit Boy flies inside the giant rocket. He enters the control room.

Captain Robo tells Super Rabbit Boy everything:

Glob Glorp was King Viking in disguise! He tricked Super Rabbit Boy into flying off into space on an endless journey. Then King Viking captured Animal Town while Super Rabbit Boy was busy in space!

Super Rabbit Boy is shocked. But he quickly jumps back into his rocket!

Can Super Rabbit Boy get back to Animal Town before it's too late?

10 HOMEWARD BOUND

Super Rabbit Boy blasts through space all the way back home.

This Level 11 rocket is so fast!

King Viking is making trouble in Animal Town. He has a giant Level 10 Robo-U.F.O.

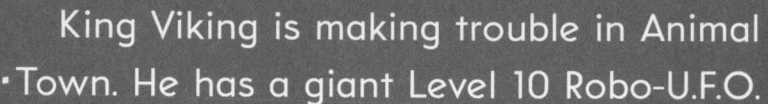

King Viking! You stinky trickster!

Super Rabbit Boy! What are you doing back?

Super Rabbit Boy blasts King Viking's Robo-U.F.O. with his Level 11 laser. King Viking goes flying. His plans have been ruined again.

Well done, Super Rabbit Boy. You saved Animal Town and space, too!

THOMAS FLINTHAM

has always loved to draw and tell stories, and now that is his job! He grew up in Lincoln, England, and studied illustration in Camberwell, London. He lives by the sea with his wife, Bethany, in Cornwall.

Thomas is the creator of Thomas Flintham's Book of Mazes and Puzzles and many other books for kids. PRESS START! is his first early chapter book series.

PRESS START!

How much do you know about
SUPER RABBIT BOY BLASTS OFF!?

Why does King Viking leave Animal Town?

There are new kinds of robots in this story. Which robot is your favorite?

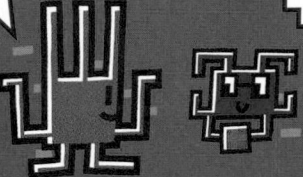

What does Super Rabbit Boy learn about King Viking on page 64? How does this news make him feel?

How does Super Rabbit Boy upgrade his rocket?

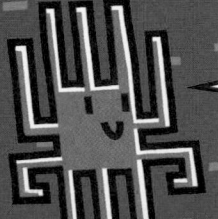

Would you want to live on a different planet? Why or why not? Write an opinion paragraph explaining your answer.

scholastic.com/branches